ishing you
ts of luck
n your first
day at school
love
from
Gayna
x x

This book belongs to

. Tommy . Hutchings. .

Written by Franzeska Ewart

Illustrated by Leonie Shearing

Language consultant: Betty Root

This is a Parragon book
This edition published in 2006

Parragon
Queen Street House
4 Queen Street
BATH BA1 1HE, UK

Printed in Indonesia

Starting School

Franzeska Ewart   Leonie Shearing

On the FIRST school day, Sadie and her mum meet
Sam and his dad.

"I'm excited," says Sadie, jumping up and down.
"I'm nervous," says Sam, holding Dad's hand tight.

Sadie's schoolbag has a picture of Cinderella on it.
Sam's schoolbag has a picture of a football.

"I've got juice," says Sadie. "And an apple."
"I've got juice too," says Sam, "and an orange ...
and biscuits ... and crisps."

Their teacher's name is Mrs Bean. She comes to greet the children and says "Hello!"

Sadie says "Bye!" to Mum. Sam says a very quiet "Bye!" to Dad. Mrs Bean says "Bye!" too. Then she takes Sam and Sadie by the hand and in they go.

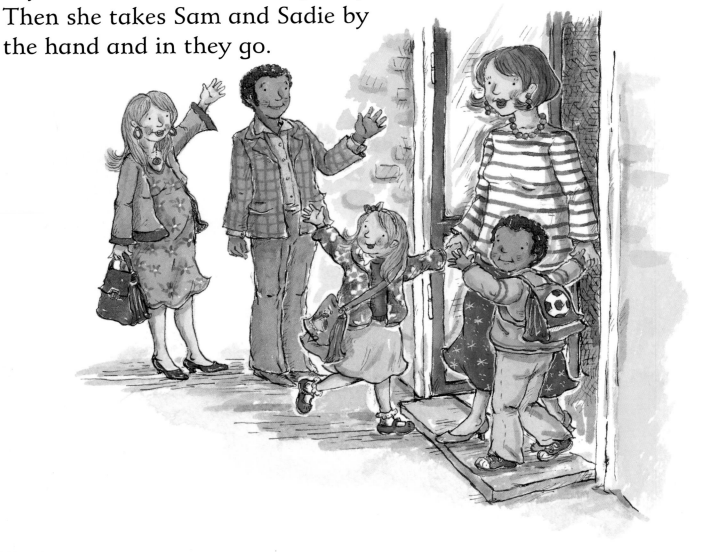

Mrs Bean puts a sticky name label onto their clothes. Above each name, there's a picture.

"Your drawer has the same picture on it," says Mrs Bean.

"And your cloakroom peg, and your special place on the shoe trolley."

Sam puts his coat on the blue lorry peg. Sadie puts hers on the carrot one.

Some children are already playing in the classroom. Sam wants to do a jigsaw. He feels a bit shy.

Sadie watches the other children. And in a cage in the corner, something watches Sadie ...

The children sit on the carpet by Mrs Bean. Now she has the cage on her knee. From under some straw, a tiny pink nose wobbles at them.

"Do you know who our special classroom friend is?" asks Mrs Bean. The children put up their hands but no one has the right answer. Mrs Bean shakes her head.

"He's a gerbil, and his name is George," says Mrs Bean. "And you've all got to look after him!"

George crawls out from under the straw and sits up.

Then the children sing a song together, to help learn each other's names.

By break-time, Sadie knows Hannah's name.

Sam knows Ben's.

Everyone knows George's.

At break-time, some big boys and girls come into the classroom.

"These are your Buddies," says Mrs Bean. "They'll help you with your coats and jackets. And if you've forgotten where the toilet is, they'll help with that too."

Sadie is pleased. She has forgotten already.

The playground is HUGE. There are games painted on the ground in bright colours.

The children eat their snacks. Sam gives a piece of orange to Ben, a biscuit to Jessica, and some crisps to Sadie.

They play hopscotch, and Joe falls over Sam.
Sadie pulls them both up. The two boys smile at her.

In the classroom Joe shows off his hurt knee. When everyone's admired it, Mrs Bean puts on a plaster. She reads a story about a bear called Barney.

"Hands up if you know what colour Barney's jumper is," she says.

Ben puts both hands up and shouts "Red!"
"Well done, Ben," says Mrs Bean. "And next time, one hand will do nicely."

The children paint pictures of Barney.

Sam gets a sticker that says: "I'm a star!"

He feels like a star.

On the SECOND school day, Mrs Bean plays a tape.

"It's Music and Movement," she says. "And first we have to warm up."

'Warm-up' is brilliant!

Hands on hips and ...

step together ...

step together.

reach up tall and ...

CLAP!

Knee up high ...

"I'm VERY warmed up!"
says Sadie.
    Everyone is as red
as Barney's jumper!

Back in the classroom, the children write some words. At first,
Sadie doesn't think she can.

Mrs Bean writes a word with her magic teacher's pen.
Then Sadie goes over the letters and writes 'cat'.

"Well done, Sadie!" says Mrs Bean.

Next, they write some numbers. At first, Sam thinks it looks too hard.

Mrs Bean writes the numbers with her magic pen. Sam goes over them. It's quite easy, really.

When dinner-time comes, the Buddies help the children to wash their hands.

They help them decide what to eat, too. There are so many choices!

"Take your time," says Mrs Bean. "Only maybe not too long ..."

Sadie has brought a packed lunch, so she doesn't have to decide.

On the THIRD school day, Mrs Bean says, "I think George is a bit smelly."

So the children help her to clean out George's cage.

"On Friday," she tells them, "one of you can take him home."

Sadie hopes it will be her!

"Today," says Mrs Bean, "we're going to paint George."

Sam thinks George looks a bit worried. (You can tell by his nose.)
"It's OK," Sam whispers. "We're only going to paint pictures
of you."

Mrs Bean's class

"Roll up your sleeves!" says Mrs Bean. She gives the children plastic aprons and they start to paint.

"We'll hang the paintings on our washing line to dry," Mrs Bean says.

Mrs Bean writes a story on Sadie's painting. Sadie can't wait to show it to Mum and Dad!

On the FOURTH school day, Mrs Bean says, "Today we're going to have a teddy bears' picnic for all your bear friends."

"There's nothing to eat!" says Sam.
"You're going to make the cakes!" says Mrs Bean. "And then you can add the icing ... and make faces on them too!"

The children put on aprons and wash their hands. Then they make the cakes.

Mrs Bean puts a name label beside each cake.

"I know everyone's name," says Sam.
"Wow!" calls Sadie. "It didn't take long!"

Then the children sit with the bears and eat their cakes. They sing a counting song.

Three little bears sitting in the forest ...

At the end of the FIFTH school day, lots of children get stickers.

"Now," says Mrs Bean, "who's going to take George home?"
She smiles at Sadie. Mrs Bean knows that Sadie would love to take George home. She gives Sadie a sticker that says: "I was a good friend". She hands her George's cage too.

Sadie is so happy, she thinks she's going to BURST!

The children line up to go home.

"I like school," says Sadie.
"I think I do too," says Sam.

George wobbles his tiny nose. He knows he does!